THE CURIOUS TRIAL OF DR. ALLEN FINE

By Joseph Shrager, MD

Published by Writers Publishing House

Paperback ISBN: 978-1-64873-422-9
Ebook ISBN: 978-1-64873-423-6

Cover design by Writers Publishing House

Printed in the United States
Prescott, Arizona

CAST OF CHARACTERS

NAME	ROLL	IDENTITY
Middle-aged woman	Beginning of story (Prologue)	MW
Arlene Motis	Wife of Plaintiff	AM
Bill Coker	Brother-in-law of Plaintiff	BC
Jack Motis	Plaintiff	JM
Dr. Allen Fine	Dermatologist-defendant	AF
Dr. Eric Vanderhoff	Dermatologist - Expert Cutaneous Lymphomas	EV
Cynthia Wils	Physician's Assistant for Dr. Fine	CW
Paul Shilita	Dr. Fine's personal lawyer/friend	PS
Insurance Man	Sets up defense for Dr. Fine (phone only)	IM
Seymour Levit	Chairman panel of 3 judges-arbitration	SL
Court Clerk	Bailiff in Arbitration Court and Court of Common Pleas	CC
Clifford Harris	Defendant's attorney/arbitration panel	CH
George Jones	Defendant's attorney/Court of Common Pleas	GJ
Dr. John Peters	Expert Witness for Dr. Fine	JP
Joseph Knight	Lawyer for plaintiff and wife	JK
Joseph Clark	Judge-Court of Common Pleas	JC
Dr. Martin Franklyn	Expert witness for Plaintiff	MF
Mrs. Binswanger	Dr. Fine's patient	MB
Howard Kurtz	Arbitration court judge (audience member)	HK
William Smithers	Arbitration court judge (audience member)	WS

Jury   Nine members of the audience come to top of stage at
the beginning of the second act. They will act as the jury
in the court of common pleas. The lawyers will present
their cases directly to the jurors.

PROLOGUE

Joseph Shrager is sitting at a table with a stack of papers in front of him.
He is reading the papers and writing notes on them. A middle-aged
woman comes in and sits across from him.

MW   Is this seat taken?

JS   No, please sit down if you like.

MW   Are you doing your taxes?

JS   No, I'm just working on a play that I hope to enter as a new
      playwright at the Prescott Center.

MW   What's it about, can I ask?

JS   Twenty-five years ago, I was a practicing dermatologist in
      Philadelphia, Pennsylvania. A man received first and second burns
      in a strong sunlamp booth due to treating him for a severe skin
      condition. He did not follow my instructions, so he was burned.
      Well, he sued me, and a strange series of events followed. That is
      what this play is all about. I call the play *The Curious Trial of Dr.
      Allen Fine*.

MW   But is that your name?

JS   No. The play tells the true story, but the names of the characters
      are changed to protect the guilty. If I used their real names, the
      lawyers would probably sue me; they are very clever. They would
      probably win.

MW   It sounds interesting. I will probably go and see it, and I will look for you there.

JS   Oh, I won't be there. I wrote the play. I know how it ends. I don't want to see the damn thing.

      (JS gets up, takes his papers, and leaves. The woman watches him leave. She has a bewildered look on her face. She turns to the audience and gives a short set of instructions.)

MW   Turn cell phones off- (usual opening remarks.)

Blackout

ACT 1

(Bill Coker rings the bell and is let into the house by his sister, Arlene Motis).

AM   How is my favorite brother, and only brother, may I add?

BC   Fine! I haven't heard from you or Jack in the past 4 four months. So, I thought I would stop over and say "Hello."

AM   Well, Jack is very depressed. You know that about a year and a half ago, Jack and two of his friends decided to start a car rental business in the Bahamas, in Freeport, to be exact. But I never told you the rest of the story.

BC   Did they go through with that plan?

AM   Well, they each put in $300,000. Jack and I had to dig deep into our savings. They used the money to buy 36 military Jeeps, which were no longer operational, and were stored in an Army warehouse. They had the Jeeps completely refurbished and painted island colors – light blue, dark blue, red, yellow, orange, and white. This was all done by a guy in Florida, who turned out to be a crook.

BC   How did they get them to Freeport?

AM   They shipped them on a boat from Maimi. Byron, one partner, was a wealthy guy with a home in Freeport. He had become friendly with Michael Mason, a Bahamian businessman who had rented a desk in the lobby of the Princess Hotel in Freeport. This is a massive hotel with over 600 rooms. The women would sit at the desk and sell bus tours of the island to guests at the hotel and anyone else on the island who wanted the tour. Byron made a deal with Michael that for $4,000 a month, these women would rent out these Jeeps for $80 a day. We hired a lawyer who took care of these details and ensured everything we did in Freeport was consistent with the law. Everything started out great. We had plenty of customers. People loved the idea of driving these colorful Jeeps around the island.

But within the next six months, things started to change. Four of our Jeeps had broken down, and it was almost impossible to get replacement parts. We took it out of service when a Jeep broke down and cannibalized it for parts.

Another large hotel was built on the island, and they built a magnificent golf course there. Business at the Princess was way off, and Michael Mason was now asking for $6,000 a month instead of his original $4,000.

One month ago, the partners decided to move our Jeeps over to Nassau, which they did. Things were looking up the first ten days we were there. Then all hell broke loose. The taxi drivers claimed we were taking away too much of their business and went on strike. The Prime Minister said we could no longer rent out Jeeps on the island, and we sold them to another car rental agency for 15 cents on the dollar. Whether we will ever see the money is another matter. Jack and I could end up losing the entire $300,000.

On top of all this, Jack has developed a terrible itching rash over his entire body. It was biopsied by a local dermatologist and proved to be a type of lymphoma where the white blood cells attack the skin, causing a severe rash and sometimes even forming tumors. It usually progresses slowly, and could take 10 to 20 years before becoming fatal. Until recently, there was no good treatment for it. Now they are trying a new approach where the doctor prescribes pills, and then 1 to 3 hours later, you go into this large lightbox where there are 36 to 42 ultraviolet light bulbs. You stay in this box for several minutes in the center of these lights three times a week. At first, you get red from these lights, then within a week, you get a dark tan. Thus far, the results have been quite encouraging. Whether this can cure the problem or send it into a temporary remission, we don't know yet. It's too new.

(Jack enters the room.)

JM   Hi Bill! I didn't know you were here.

BC   Hi! I haven't seen you or Arlene in a long time. So, I thought I would stop over.

JM   I suppose Arlene told you what is going on in the Bahamas?

BC   She did. How badly is that going to hurt you?

JM   Even before the Bahamas, Arlene and I were thinking of selling this large house, moving to a smaller one, or even going into an apartment. Now we may have to sell this house and go less expensive. We took a big hit.

BC   Arlene also told me that you were having health problems.

JM   I went to a local dermatologist for my rash. After running some tests, he recommended I see a doctor at Hahnemann Hospital in Philadelphia, specializing in diseases like mine. But let's not talk about that right now. Come into the kitchen. We'll have some beer and pizza, and I have some new jokes I want to try on you.

(Jack and Bill leave the room, talking to each other in a low voice.)

JM   (Enters the kitchen with Bill – talks in normal voice.) Bill, would you like mushrooms on your pizza? The beer is in the refrigerator, help yourself.

BC   Thanks, yes, I'll take some mushrooms.

JM   Tom Lewis is ranked one of the top ten high school wrestlers in the United States at 180 pounds. He is accepted into the University of Oklahoma on a full tuition paid wrestling scholarship. His freshman year, he wins all of his matches. Bigger and stronger at the end of his second year, he wins the intercollegiate heavyweight championship. By the completion of his fourth year, he weighs 280 pounds, and represents the United States in the Olympics as a super heavyweight. There he defeats all his opponents in record time. After the Olympics, he turns professional. For the next 18 months, he remains undefeated, at the end of which time he challenges the world super heavyweight champion for the championship belt. Vladimer Pigortney is no slouch. He is undefeated over the past 12 years and is world renowned for his lightning-fast application of the Russian pretzel hold. This is a move in which your opponent is twisted into the shape of a pretzel and cannot escape. Pigortney accepts the challenge. The match begins, and for 45 minutes neither man can gain an advantage over the other. Then suddenly Pigortney makes a surprise move that catches Tom off guard, and then suddenly Tom finds himself trapped in the famous Russian pretzel hold. Tom cannot move, but somehow manages to free his neck so that he can now twist his head. He looks around and sees two big hairy balls. Using all his strength, he stretches over and bites them as hard as he can. The Russian flies out of the ring, hitting his head sharply on the edge of a wooden chair. Unable to get back into the ring by the count of 10, he loses the match. Tom Lewis is interviewed after the match and is asked by the TV announcer how he managed to be the only wrestler to free himself from the pretzel hold.

He replies: "It's amazing how strong you get when you bite your own balls".

BS   Ha, ha, ha. That's a great one. I'll have to remember it. By the way, I noticed Arlene put on a couple of pounds.

JM   Yes. She's upset about my health and our financial situation.

       Some people lose weight when worried. She tends to eat more

       when she's upset. She also can't exercise because of her bad back.

BS   I have a joke for you. Frank goes into Mike's Bar and Grill on

       First Avenue. After consuming a few drinks, he announces to the

       bartender that he wants to buy a beer for everyone in the bar,

       except for that Jewish guy sitting by himself at the end of the bar.

       All the patrons come up one by one to thank Frank. The last one

       up is the Jewish guy sitting by himself, who seems quite pleased.

       Frank is somewhat surprised, but doesn't say anything. Twenty

       five minutes later, after three more drinks, Frank again tells the

       bartender to give everyone a free drink on him, except for the Jew

       sitting at the and of the bar. Again, one by one, the patrons thank

       Frank for his generosity. Again, the last one is the Jew, who seems

       very pleased, and thanks Frank vociferously for his generosity.

       Frank is puzzled and turns to the bartender. Why is that man

       thanking me? I didn't offer to buy him a drink. Oh, answers the

       bartender, that's Mike Cohen. He owns the bar.

JM   That's good. I didn't expect that ending.

(Arlene Motis comes into the kitchen.)

AM   I thought I would join you. Is that pizza I smell?

JM   Forget it! You've had plenty to eat for lunch and you don't need to

       put on any more weight.

AM   That's not fair. You know that since I got that herniated disc, I
        haven't been able to exercise.

JM   Yeah, and our sex life has gone down the toilet. Don't forget that.

BC   Well, I'll be going now. My wife is probably wondering where I
        am.

(Scene shifts to the office of Dr. Allen Fine, a well-respected
dermatologist in Philadelphia.)

(Cynthia Wils, the physician's assistant who works with him, enters the
office.)

CW   Dr. Fine, Dr. Vanderhoff is on the phone regarding one of his
        patients.

AF   Tell him that I will be with him in just a minute. Tell Mrs. French
        to finish the prescribed pills, apply the cortisone cream twice
        daily, and make an appointment for two weeks. If she is better, she
        can cancel the appointment.

(Takes phone.)

        Hi Eric, what's up?

EV   Hi Allen. Mr. Jack Motis is in my office. He is a patient with
        cutaneous T-cell lymphoma referred by a dermatologist in
        Delaware for PUVA light treatments. Recent reports in JAMA
        have indicated that increasing the number of treatments from 3 to
        4 times a week gives longer, more lasting periods of remission,

and possibly, in some cases, a cure. He wants me to take over the case and start a more aggressive approach. However, tomorrow I'm leaving for an international dermatology meeting in Prague and won't return for three weeks. I want you to know I have already treated several patients on this new schedule. We gave them treatments on Monday, Wednesday, Friday and Saturday. We reduced the dose of Psoralens orally that we gave 2 hours before each light treatment, and reduced the duration of each light treatment from 2 ½ minutes to 1 ½ minutes. So far, none of our patients have been burned by the lights, but they have gotten red and then developed a dark tan, just as we had hoped. The results have been dramatic. Would you be willing to start him on that regimen until I return?

AF   I would be glad to. Could you ask him to call my office tomorrow to schedule an appointment? Cynthia Wils, my physician's assistant, and I will review the procedure with him and begin his treatments later this week. When you get back, we will send him back to you to complete his therapy course. In the meantime, have a great trip.

EV   Thanks. I will see you when I get back.

AF   So long.

(Hangs up phone and talks to Cynthia Wils.)

Did you hear that conversation, Cynthia? Dr. Vanderhoff is a world authority on cutaneous T-cell lymphoma. I'm delighted he is referring this case to us for PUVA light treatments while he is away. There are 7 or 8 other dermatologists in Philadelphia with PUVA boxes to whom he could have sent him.

(Monday – Dr. Fine's office. Cynthia Wils, the physician's assistant, talks to the patient, Jack Motis.)

CW   Hello, I'm Ms. Wils, the physician's assistant. I will review your medical history with you, and then go over what cutaneous T-cell lymphoma is about, and we will begin the treatments for this disease. When Dr. Vanderhoff returns in 3 ½ weeks, you will return to him to complete your treatments. How is your general health?

JM   Fine!

CW   Are you taking any medications or allergic to any drugs?

JM   I'm not taking any medications at present. I am not allergic to any meds that I know of.

CW   Do you have any problems with your heart, lungs, kidneys, blood, or nervous system?

JM   No!

CW   Who is your family physician?

JM   Dr. Frank Jared, but I'm not seeing him for anything at present. Can you tell me about my disease? Is it life-threatening, and how do you plan to treat it?

CW   Did your first dermatologist go into any details about your disease?

JM   Not really. He always seemed in a big hurry. He took a biopsy and
        told me that I had cancer of the white blood cells, which were
        affecting my skin and giving me the rash. He transferred me to Dr.
        Vanderhoff, who referred me here to get started on my treatment.

CW   OK. I will start by telling you about your condition and how we
        will treat it. You have a type of cancer of the white blood cells that
        form in the thymus gland and are referred to as T-cells. These
        enter the bloodstream and, from there, into the skin. Here, they
        cause rashes, and when they aggregate in large numbers, they may
        cause skin tumors. These rashes usually progress slowly, taking
        years before they become lethal.

Until recently, treatment was not
very effective in controlling the
progress of the disease. Over the past
several years, a new treatment type
was developed, which looks very
promising. PUVA boxes have been
built and sold to dermatologists.
These boxes look like large
telephone booths, but are round

instead of square. We have one in the next room. Come with me,
I'll show you.

(JM goes into the next room with Cynthia, where he sees this PUVA box.)

JM   What is it supposed to do?

(Cynthia opens the "box.")

CW   As you can see, there are 36 tall fluorescent lights. Each is 7 feet high and perpendicular to the ground. They surround the patient once he or she steps into the box. These are not the usual fluorescent lights we think of. They give off a wavelength of ultraviolet light called ultraviolet A light, higher than the ultraviolet lights you are familiar with, which give off ultraviolet B light. The A light primarily causes you to tan, while the B light causes you to get red and is more likely to give you a burn.

Notice surrounding the patient is a handrail. This keeps him in the center of the light, preventing the patient from getting more light on one side of the body than the other. It prevents him from getting burned on that side of the body. The rails also prevent them from slipping or falling.

JM   Why do they call this a PUVA box?

CW   One to two hours before entering the box, the patient takes a medication called Psoralen. This medication causes the patient to be more sensitive to the light and get a stronger, deeper tan. It also increases the reddening effect the patient gets with the first several treatments. The first letter of the name of the drug is a "P." The remainder of the word UVA stands for the light emitted from the bulbs. Hence, PUVA box. You will come to the office every Monday, Wednesday, Friday, and Saturday for the next three weeks for these light treatments. Two hours before you get here, you will take 2 Psoralen tablets. After your treatments here are completed, you will go back to Dr. Vanderhoff for final instructions. OK?

JM   It sounds good to me. Should I be on the lookout for any dangers or side effects?

CW   Yes. I will review the list of problems that could occur, and I will give you a medical release to sign should any of these problems occur.

JM   (Patient reads the list aloud.)

For the treatment to be effective, the intensity of the lights must be strong enough for your skin to turn pink-red, and, subsequently, turn dark tan. If the intensity or length of exposure is too strong, the patient could get 2nd or even 3rd-degree burns. Third-degree burns, however, would be very unusual. Second and third-degree burns would include redness and blistering. In second-degree burns, the blisters would last a week to 10 days before drying up and leaving no permanent marks or scars. Third-degree burns include blisters and scabs that could persist up to and beyond two weeks. Permanent scarring would follow, and pain and discomfort could last for weeks or months. I am not aware that permanent scarring from PUVA has been reported.

Other problems that could occur include slipping in the PUVA box. That's why you must hold onto the handrails. You must stand straight and not slouch. You must remain in the center of the lightbox to avoid over-exposure to the lights on only one side of your body. A stand-straight sign is posted, which you will see when you step into the box. Eye protection is important. You will purchase from us a set of powerful sunglasses that will protect you 100% from ultraviolet A and ultraviolet B rays. You are to wear them at all times from 7 a.m. to 6 p.m., especially when going into the lightbox for the duration of the treatments. Nausea, vomiting, and diarrhea can occur from the medication but are uncommon. If these side effects occur, contact us immediately, and we will tell you what to do. If any other medical problems occur, contact us. We may discontinue the therapy until we think we can safely resume the treatments.

Any questions? If not, please sign at the bottom indicating that you are aware of possible dangers and wish to begin the therapy.

JM   What happens if I don't want to sign?

CW   We can't treat you, and you will have to go to another dermatologist or wait for Dr. Vanderhoff to return.

JM   I'll be happy to sign it.

(JM signs form. Dr. Fine enters the office.)

AF   I'm Dr. Fine. Did Miss Wils answer all your questions and explain what we are about to do?

JM   Yes, she did. She was very informative.

AF   OK. We will begin your treatments this Wednesday. You will come in every Wednesday, Friday, Saturday, and Monday for the next 2 1/2 to 3 weeks, after which time you will return to Dr. Vanderhoff to conclude your treatments. Here is a bottle of Psoralen tablets. You will take the tablets two hours before each scheduled treatment. Remember to wear these sunglasses.

(Dr. Fine hands him the sunglasses.)

JM   Thank you.

AF   I want to see you in follow-up before your second treatment on Friday.

JM   Thank you. I'll be here tomorrow for my first treatment.

AF   Fine. Bye. Make your follow-up appointments with the receptionist.

(Wednesday morning, JM comes in for his first appointment.)

CW   Hello. Did you take the tablets?

JM   Yes.

CW   Have you been wearing the special glasses we gave you?

JM   I took my first tablets and have been wearing my glasses continuously.

CW   OK. Step into the PUVA box.

(She opens the door to the box.)

        Step in carefully so as not to trip. Stand up straight in the middle of the box and hold onto the metal railings. Now, close your eyes.

(JM enters the box and closes the door. Lights go on, and 1 ½ minutes later, the lights go off. JM opens the door and comes out of the box.)

CW   Make an appointment for Friday for your next treatment. Dr. Fine will be there. If you have any questions, we will answer them at that time.

(Friday, JM arrives at the office and speaks to Cynthia.)

JM   I would like to see the doctor.

(She gets Dr. Fine)

AF   Any problems?

JM   My skin is red, and I have sore blisters on my butt from the light treatment.

AF   Get undressed and put on this gown with the opening to the back.

(Dr. Fine examines his back, the back of his legs and thighs, and his buttocks. He also looks at his front, chest, abdomen, and private areas.

15

AF	Your skin is red – a first-degree burn. That is what we want. The blisters on your buttocks are the result of the second-degree burn, but it's not a big deal. They should heal in 5 or 6 days. The pain will disappear, and you will not have scars. We will hold off on further treatments until next Monday. In the meantime, I'll prescribe a mild cortisone lotion, which should make your skin feel better and heal more quickly. Apply it twice daily.

(Next Monday at the office of Dr. Fine. JM does not show up for his light treatment).

CW	Dr Fine, I called him, and he said that he was seeing another dermatologist. He sounded very rude on the phone.

(Three weeks later, in Dr. Fine's office.)

AF	I got a letter from a lawyer who states that he represents Jack Motis. It seems that Mr. Motis is suing us. His lawyer asks for a copy of our records and that we turn this letter over to our insurance carrier so they may contact him. Would you have Brenda take care of that?

CW	That jerk! I will take care of it myself.

AF	Mr. Motis is asking our carrier for $25,000 to settle the case for the burns he got on his butt. I'm not going to agree with that. He signed a medical release. He knew we were using high-intensity lights and had to get some burning response for positive results. He knew that there was a risk of getting a second-degree burn. I'm sure his blisters healed quickly, not leaving him with any residual scarring or pain.

I'll also bet his skin rash has improved, even though he only had one treatment. He should have continued with these light treatments. By this time, the redness would have progressed to a dark tan, and the T-cell lymphoma would have improved. He could have even kept his undershorts on if he was worried about getting more blisters. Once he started to get a deep tan, the tan would prevent further blistering.

(Seven days later, the phone rings and CW answers it.)

CW   Dr. Fine, a man from your medical malpractice insurance company, is on the phone.

(Dr. Fine answers the phone.)

AF   Hello! Yes, this is Dr. Allen Fine. Listen, we discussed with Mr. Motis all the possible problems that could result from these treatments, none of which were super serious. He stated that he was willing to accept these risks and signed a medical release saying he would accept them. I saw his blisters shortly after his first treatment. They were mild second-degree burns on his buttocks, which I am sure healed entirely within 5-7 days. They are not going to leave scars. As a matter of fact, we need some burn to get his problem resolved. Will his problem be resolved entirely or permanently? I don't know, but it is the standard treatment for his condition.

What annoys me the most is that he stopped his treatment with me. Even if he gets no more treatments elsewhere, he should see some positive results from his treatment.

(Insurance man on phone.)

IM   He wants $25,000 to settle the case. I suggest you give it to him.
We will cover it, and he will be off your back.

AF   No! I will not agree to give him $25,000 for his pain and suffering.
He signed a release. I would rather face him in court. Keep in touch
and let me know what is happening.

IM   OK.

(Paul Shalita's office two years later. Case has not yet come to trial.)

PS   No, I do not think this is a good time to bring a junior partner into
your office. More partnerships do not work out than those that do.
We may be heading into a recession, which would work against
increasing the number of doctors in your office now.

Also, I reviewed your income versus your business expenses. It
makes no sense to keep two offices. You have two rents, two office
staff, and limited time for each office.

AF   That's why I was thinking of bringing in a partner. He would work
in one office while I worked in the other.

PS   That's a possibility, but I think it is risky. You are again stuck with
two offices if you and your partner break up. It takes 45 minutes to
get to your office in town, and 10 minutes to reach your office in
Abington. You are completely booked in your Abington office. I
think it's financially foolish to stay in town.

AF   I know you are right, and I will give up my center city office when my lease runs out. But I will miss my center city patients, whom I have come to like and respect.

PS   My wife was talking to Diane this past Friday and your wife told Myrna that your trial over the burn is coming up in 2 weeks.

AF   Yes, it will be an arbitration hearing in front of three lawyers. Each side, however, has two weeks to seek a retrial in the Court of Common Pleas. Why would my insurance company accept an arbitration hearing like that? That would be a complete waste of time and money. If the plaintiff loses, he could take it to the next level, the Court of Common Pleas.

PS   In Pennsylvania, the law states: "... that if the demand by the plaintiff is below $50,000, it must go to an arbitration hearing first."

AF   I am having second thoughts about the whole thing. Maybe I should have had my insurance company pay Mr. Motis the $25,000 and get it off my back.

PS   I told you that right from the beginning.

AF   I got a phone call from Clifford Harris. He will be the lawyer representing me. I will meet with him on Friday to review my case. What do you know about him?

PS   I've heard of him. He has a good reputation.

AF   By the way, I got a letter from my malpractice carrier. In 3 months, they are going out of business. They will continue to cover me for this trial. My contract with them will expire in December of this year, and they will continue to be responsible for any malpractice lawsuits resulting from my actions up until then. However, they will not represent me. I was assigned to Amalgamated Protective Malpractice Insurance Company for any such cases.

PS   They don't have the greatest reputation. They pick their defense lawyers on a bidding basis. They print a resume of the case and send the resume to any interested defense lawyers. These guys bid on the cases, and the job is usually given to the lawyer, who will work for the smallest amount of money. The better companies have their stable of lawyers who only work for them.

AF   I guess that means if my case goes to the Court of Common Pleas, I'll get a lousy lawyer to defend me.

PS   Not necessarily, but that is often the case. You can hire your own lawyer if you want to.

AF   Too expensive. Oh, I almost forgot. I bought a small gift for you, an ancient Egyptian apple pie.

PS   I never heard of it.

AF   Oh, you know, the kind that mummy used to make. I'll send it over to you. HA, ha, ha!

(Two weeks later.)

First trial – 10 a.m. January 30, 1998, at 1605 Chestnut St., Philadelphia, PA. This is the arbitration the plaintiff, the defendant, and their lawyers agreed upon.

(Three men enter the courtroom and sit next to one another at a long table facing the audience in the arbitration courtroom. The man in the middle speaks.)

SL	Hi, my name is Seymour Levit. I am the chairman of this panel of 3 judges. The men on each side of me and I are attorneys from Philadelphia, and we shall decide the guilt or innocence of the defendant. The rules of the American Arbitration Association govern us. To my right is Mr. Howard Kurtz, and to my left is Mr. William Smithers. If either side does not agree with our decision, he will have 14 days to appeal for a retrial in the Court of Common Pleas of Philadelphia located at city hall. If the defendant and the plaintiff choose not to appeal, then they will abide by our decision. Mr. Joseph Knight is the lawyer for the plaintiff, and Mr. Clifford Harris is the lawyer for the defendant. Mr. Knight, would you please call the plaintiff to the witness stand?

JK	In this trial. Mr. Jack Motis claims damages from burns suffered from a sunlamp treatment given in March, 1995. This treatment was given in the office of and under the direction of Dr. Allen Fine for a type of lymphoma that invades the skin. Both Mr. Motis and Dr. Fine are here today. The arbitration will be conducted in accordance with and under the rules set forth by the American Arbitration Association. I'll start by saying that my client, Mr. Jack Motis, has a chronic skin condition that, after numerous tests, has proven to be a type of lymphoma that attacks the skin. It is cutaneous T-cell lymphoma, C-T-C-L. I want to call Mr. Motis to the stand.

(Mr. Motis comes up to the witness stand.)

CC   Mr. Motis, please put your right hand on the Bible. Do you swear to tell the truth, the whole truth, and nothing but the truth?

JM   I do.

JK   Mr. Motis, please tell us in your own words what happened in 1995 when you sought help from Dr. Allen Fine for your skin condition.

JM   When I went to Dr. Fine's office, I saw his assistant, Ms. Cynthia Wils.

JK   Was she a doctor?

JM   She said she was a physician's assistant. She talked to me about my problem and said it would be a chronic one that would probably not kill me. She said it would worsen over time, but that the good news was that a recent new therapy had been developed using high-intensity ultraviolet A light and certain pills that I would take before the light treatments. I would come in 4 days a week for these treatments. They would be given in a booth that looked like a round telephone booth and contained 36 ultraviolet lights, which would surround me. I was told that my skin would turn red from the first and second treatments but then turn a dark tan within a few days, and my rash would gradually fade. She said these treatments have proven very effective over the past several years. I started the treatment, and within 2-3 days, my skin became very red, and painful blisters appeared over my buttocks on both sides. I work as a real estate appraiser for several banks and must drive a lot. Because of the blisters, I had to cut down a lot on my driving, and my income went down.

JK   Did Dr. Fine tell you that you might get painful blisters over your buttocks?

JM   Dr. Fine never really told me much of anything. He never said that I could get tender, painful blisters anywhere. I had a hard time sitting even in my living room. The blisters started to ooze after 3-4 days, and I soiled my pants. I felt very embarrassed.

JK   How long did it take for the blisters to heal?

JM   Almost ten days, but even after they healed, I had pain sitting down.

JK   Did you go back to Dr. Fine after the blisters healed?

JM   No. I was afraid to. I was worried that he might want to restart the treatments and that I might get more burns. He told me that to get the desired benefits from the light treatments, the light would have to be strong enough to cause redness. Several months later, I went to see Dr. Vanderhoff. He restarted the treatments and cleared my skin.

JK   Did the rest of your skin turn red and burn like Dr. Fine's treatment?

JW   Yes. It was uncomfortable for a while, but not like the blisters.

JK   I have no further questions.

SL   Mr. Harris, would you like to question the witness?

CH   Yes, your honor. Mr. Motis, after the blisters healed, and the redness started to turn into a tan, did you notice any improvement in your skin condition?

JM   There was itching, and I did notice some improvement.

CH   Dr. Fine said the itching had been very severe when you first came to his office. Is that true?

JM   Yes.

CH   And then you stopped the treatments for how long? And did the itching and rash worsen again?

JM   The rash and itching worsened after I had been off the treatment for 1-2 months.

CH   Am I correct that if you had not seen improvement after only one successful treatment, you would not have restarted these treatments with Dr. Vanderhoff?

JM   I wouldn't exactly call this one treatment successful.

CH   Please answer the question. Would you have restarted the treatments when the condition flared?

JM   That is correct.

CH   Did Ms. Wils tell you that you might have side effects from these treatments, and did she give you a sheet of paper that listed these side effects?

JM   Yes.

CH   Did she ask you to read that list of possible side effects and then sign the paper, which she called a medical release, if you were willing to accept these risks?

JM   I don't recall her saying that it was called a release, but I didn't think they would treat me if I didn't sign the paper.

CH   Is this the paper you signed, and is this your signature at the bottom?

JM   Yes.

CH   Would you read the list of possible side effects?

JM   1. Injuries - slipping and falling inside the lightbox. This can be avoided or minimized by tightly holding onto the handrails.

2. First and second-degree burns from the intense light treatments. This can often be avoided by standing straight inside the lightbox. You should stand in the center of the box, equidistant from all the surrounding bulbs. You should not slouch or bend over if possible.

3. Nausea, vomiting, or diarrhea from the Psoralen tablets.

4. Vision damage from UVA lights – avoided by wearing special sunglasses that protect you 100% from UVA and UVB light.

During the weeks of treatment, you should wear glasses continuously indoors and outdoors from 7 a.m. until evening.

5. If you experience any unusual health abnormalities, contact us immediately.

CH So you knew that you ran certain risks, including burns to your skin, damage to your eyes, etc.? Yet you agreed to have these PUVA treatments because of the severity of your skin problem?

JM Yes.

CH I have no further questions. I have no further witnesses.

SL In that case, we will discuss your claims and notify you of our decision in the next ten days, as in accordance with the agreement signed by you and the American Arbitration Association. If either party wishes to contest the verdict, you may apply for a retrial in the Philadelphia Court of Common Pleas within 14 days. After 14 days, the decision reached by our panel becomes final and binding.

(Dr. Allen Fine and Paul Shalita on the phone at Dr. Fine's office.)

PS Did you finally get the verdict from the Arbitration panel?

AF About ten days later, I got a registered letter saying that they had found me not liable.

PS Well, it's February 5th, and he still has four days to appeal the verdict. I don't think they will. By the way, there was a notice in the business section of the Philadelphia Inquirer that your medical malpractice insurance company was officially going out of business in the next two months. That means you will be assigned to another malpractice insurance company. You will get a letter notifying you of the details. You don't have to be concerned, OK? Take it easy, and let me know if you hear anything more.

AF   Goodbye.

(Paul Shalita calls Dr. Fine 4 weeks later.)

AF   Hi Paul. What's up?

PS   The reason I'm calling is two-fold. A client of mine just gave me four tickets to the Sixers game with the Celtics on March 5. They are in the third row, center court. Would you and Diane like to go with me and Myrna? Great game, great seats, and free tickets!

AF   That sounds great, but let me check with Diane first. If we go with you, we can stop at Villa De Roma first for dinner, on me. It's the best Italian Restaurant in South Philly. Cuz is the chef there. He's an old patient of mine, and he'll take good care of us.

PS   Great! My other question was whether Mr. Motis ever filed for a retrial.

AF   On February 7, he filed one day before the option lapsed. I got a notice four days ago.

PS   Did you inform your insurance company?

AF   I've been assigned to a new insurance company, Amalgamated Protective. I called them immediately. They're going to get me a lawyer, and they will call me.

(Seven days later, Dr. Fine calls Paul Shalita again.)

AF   I got a call from George Jones today. He's the lawyer who is going to represent me in the burn case. I'm going to meet with him next Tuesday.

PS   OK. I know nothing about him. I'll get back to you if I learn anything.

(Allen Fine meets with George Jones in Dr. Fine's office five days later.)

GJ   I got the records of your arbitration trial, and I'm reviewing them now. In the meantime, I see that your trial will be held in room 422, Court of Common Pleas, City Hall, Philadelphia, on March 23 at 10 a.m.

AF   OK. Come with me to my physician's assistant's office. I want to talk to you for a minute about several aspects of this case. The cleaning staff is here to straighten out my office.

(They leave the room, talking to each other in low tones.)

AF   Is there anything else you want to tell me or ask me?

GJ   We will need an expert dermatologist to testify on your behalf. Is there anyone you recommend?

AF	Yes. Dr. John Peters is a dermatologist who has an office in Florham Park, New Jersey. He is a very bright guy – an Assistant Professor of dermatology on the staff at the University of Pennsylvania. I'll get you his exact address and phone number. Does Mr. Motis have a dermatologist?

GJ	Yes. They have a dermatologist from Vineland, New Jersey. He treats psoriasis, C-T-C-L, and vitiligo patients with PUVA light therapy as you do. He advertises in a bi-monthly newspaper put out by a bunch of trial lawyers. He is willing to testify against other dermatologists if the price is right.

AF	I know plenty of other guys like that. I'll see you on March 28 at 9:30 a.m.

GJ	Room 422 at City Hall in Philadelphia. Here's my card.

(He hands him his business card and waves goodbye.)

ACT 2

(Scene – Court of Common Pleas – Room 422 – City Hall 10 a.m.)

9 members of the audience come on stage and take their seats in the jury box.

CC   This is Court of Common Pleas, Room 422, City Hall – Philadelphia PA. Judge Joseph L. Clark presiding. All rise.

(Everyone stands - Judge Clark enters the room and takes a seat behind the bench.)

JC   Everyone, please be seated. Mr. Knight, please explain the reason for this trial and call the plaintiff to the witness stand.

(Everyone sits.)

JK   This is a case in which a man, Jack Motis, had a severe rash over his entire body for about five months. He sought the help of a dermatologist in Philadelphia by the name of Allen Fine. Dr. Fine started him on a relatively new treatment for his rash, utilizing the taking of certain pills followed by exposure to high-intensity ultraviolet lights. After only one treatment, Mr. Motis suffered first and second-degree burns over his body. The cause of the rash was a type of lymphoma that affected the white blood cells, causing them to attack the skin. He claims that his dermatologist, Dr. Allen Fine, was negligent in administering the light treatment, causing him to suffer great discomfort and resulting in a significant loss of income. His wife of only six months at the time is also suing Dr. Fine, claiming that his burns prevented the sexual consortium that exists in the normal relationship between husband and wife. She is asking for $25,000 in damages. He is asking for $150,000 in damages.

You may never have heard of his skin condition. It is known as cutaneous T-cell lymphoma or C-T-C-L. During this trial, you will come to know more about this disease and its treatment than 99.9% of the adult U.S. population.

As I said, the plaintiffs are Mr. Jack Motis and Mrs. Gail Motis. The defendant is the physician, Dr. Allen Fine. I am the lawyer representing the plaintiffs, Mr. and Mrs. Jack Motis. My name is Joseph Knight, and the attorney for Dr. Fine, the defendant, is George Jones.

JC   Mr. Knight, will you please call your first witness?

JK   Mr. Motis, will you please take the stand?

BALIFF   Please place your right hand on the Bible. Do you solemnly swear to tell the truth, the whole truth, and nothing but the truth, so help you God?

JM   I do.

JK   Could you explain to the jury what happened on February 14, 1995, when you went to Dr. Fine's office for treatment of your skin condition?

JM   I had had this severe skin condition, which was getting worse and was very itchy. I had been biopsied and told that it was a type of lymphoma cancer that invades the skin over the entire body. I was referred to a dermatologist specializing in this disease at Hahnemann Hospital in Philadelphia. He could not see me for 3-6 weeks and referred me to Dr. Fine to begin special ultraviolet light treatments for C-T-C-L, which was the name of my condition. The Physician's Assistant in Dr. Fine's office told me it was a slowly progressing disease in 95% of the patients. I could live with it for another 10 to 20 years. On rare occasions, it could become aggressive and lead to the formation of cancerous tumors, or even become fatal.

She explained that a treatment regimen had recently been developed utilizing ultraviolet A light given in a special light box. These treatments would be given every Monday, Wednesday, Friday, and Saturday every week for 3-4 weeks. At first, your skin would turn pink, then over a period of days it would become dark tan. She said that the early results were very encouraging and, in some cases, very dramatic.

JK   Did you see Dr. Fine?

JM   He came into the room for a few minutes. He asked whether I had any questions. Then he had me schedule appointments to come into the office to get started on my treatments. I got my first treatment that Wednesday, and by Friday, my skin had become pink, and blisters had formed over my buttocks. They were painful.

JK   Had Dr. Fine told you that you might get burned with painful blisters?

JM   Dr. Fine seemed to be in a big hurry. He only spent a few minutes with me. He had not warned me about getting painful blisters on my skin.

JK   How long did the pain and the blisters last?

JM   The blisters lasted 7 to 10 days, I would say. But the pain and tenderness in the buttocks lasted probably three months. I had a hard time sitting, and it was hard for me to have a normal sexual relationship with my wife.

JK   Did this pain also affect your income?

JM   I'm a real estate appraiser. I worked for banks in the Philadelphia and Jersey areas. I couldn't sit in a car for any prolonged period of time. Instead of seeing 6 to 10 houses a day, I was lucky if I could drive to 2 or 3. My income was severely reduced. We had to sell our home and move into a small apartment because of my burns.

In Jersey there are two banks that I worked for. Sometimes, I would have to drive over roads with rocks and stones. It was too painful for me. Those two banks wound up firing me and hiring other appraisers.

JK   How much were you paid for each appraisal?

JM   That depended on the size of the home, the distance I had to travel, and other factors. By the way, I had to turn down some jobs because I could not travel long distances. In answer to your question, I usually get between $250 and $600 for each appraisal.

JK   So you lost quite a bit of money over that three-month period?

JM   That's why we had to move to an apartment. I also had to sell my Mercedes and buy an older Chevy with 60,000 miles on it.

JK   Did you ever go back to Dr. Fine after you got burned?

JM   Absolutely not. Several months later, I went back and saw Dr. Vanderhoff at Hahnemann Hospital, and he restarted the PUVA light treatments. This time I had good results.

JK   Thank you. I have no more questions.

JC   Mr. Jones, this is your time to question the witness

GJ   Yes.

(JM stays in the witness chair.)

GJ   Mr. Motis, were you ever given a paper to sign prior to starting your light treatments?

JM   Yes.

GJ   Did this paper list the side effects that could result from getting those treatments? And did it explain how you might avoid these side effects if you followed the instructions given in this paper?

JM   That was 4-5 years ago. I forgot what was written on the paper.
Besides, they would not have given me the treatments if I didn't
sign the paper.

GJ   Is this the paper that you signed prior to your treatments? And is
this your signature at the bottom of the paper?

JM   Yes.

GJ   Would you please read this paper aloud to the jury members?

(Hands paper to Mr. Motis.)

JM   Top line in big letters - MEDICAL RELEASE.

JK   Your honor, I object. A Medical Release takes a patient's right to
sue away from him or her. It is not a legal or permissible
document. It should have been titled "Informed Medical Consent".

JC   Objection sustained. This document cannot be presented as
evidence.

(Judge to the jury.)

JC   Forget that you ever saw or heard of this medical release. Its
contents are not of legal status in this case.

(Judge turns to George Jones.)

JC   You are not to allude to this document at any time in this trial.
Please proceed.

GJ   Mr. Motis, did Ms. Wils, the physician's assistant, discuss the
        possible side effects with you and the possible ways to avoid
        them?

JM   I don't recall that she did.

GJ   I have no more questions.

(Mr. Motis and Mr. Jones go back to their seats. Dr. Fine is sitting next to
Mr. Jones. Seemingly irritated, he addresses Mr. Jones.)

AF   Just because Mr. Motis moved into a smaller residence and bought
        a cheaper car does not mean he had a bad year financially. Isn't it
        standard procedure to obtain copies of his tax returns for the year
        of the accident and the years before and after the accident?

GJ   I did get those copies of his tax returns for those years. In 1994, he
        had a great year and paid $40,000 in taxes. In 1996, he paid
        $28,000 in taxes. In 1995, the year of the burns, he paid no taxes.
        Did you really expect me to point that out to the jury?

(No answer from Dr. Fine.)

JC   Mr. Knight, would you please call your next witness?

JK   Will Dr. Martin Franklin, please take the stand.

(Dr. Franklin takes the stand.)

BALIFF   Please put your right hand on the Bible. Do you swear to tell
            the truth and nothing but the truth, so help you God?

MF   I do.

JK   Dr. Franklin, what is your occupation?

MF   I am a Board-Certified Dermatologist practicing dermatology in Vineland, New Jersey.

JK   How long have you been practicing, and where did you learn your profession?

MF   I went to medical school and took my residency at Temple University and Hospital in Philadelphia. I have been practicing dermatology for over ten years.

JK   Do you treat patients with C-T-C-L?

MF   Yes, I have a PUVA box and have been treating patients with C-T-C-L, psoriasis, and vitiligo with PUVA light therapy for the past three years.

JK   Did you have occasion to treat Mr. Motis?

MF   No, I never treated Mr. Motis. I am here as an expert witness only.

JK   Dr. Franklin, do you have to burn the skin almost to the point of causing blisters in order to clear the rash?

MF   No, but you do have to increase the intensity of the light sufficiently to make the skin a deep pink. In several days, the pink will turn into a dark tan.

JK   How do you control the intensity of the light?

MF   The intensity of the light is controlled by the period of time the
      skin has been exposed to the light, and by the distance from the
      that skin where the light is placed. If you halve the distance, you
      quadruple the dose of light. The intensity is also increased by the
      amount of the Psoralen medication the patient takes prior to the
      light treatment.

JK   So you can control the amount of the medication and the time of
      the exposure. It would be difficult to manipulate the lightbox to
      change the distance between the light and the skin.

MF   Correct.

JK   Could the blisters on the buttocks have been avoided by
      shortening the time of the exposure or giving less Psoralen
      medication to the patient?

MF   Correct.

JK   Why did Mr. Motis get blisters only on his buttocks and not over
      the rest of his body?

MF   I understand that Mr. Motis had been to the Bahamas about three
      weeks before he started his treatments. Most of his skin had gotten
      tan. However, his swimming trunks had prevented his buttocks
      from getting tan. The tan was starting to fade, but was still
      sufficient to protect his body from burning. His buttocks were
      white and still vulnerable to the lights from the PUVA box.

JK   Could the burns have been prevented had Mr. Motis been told to apply a good sunscreen to his buttocks or by telling him to keep his undershorts on during the treatments?

MF   Definitely. I would have preferred sunscreen lotion to keeping on shorts.

JK   Based on the history as you know it, how bad were these burns?

MF   The redness over his trunk and extremities was due to first-degree burns. The blisters over his buttocks could have been second or third-degree burns.

JK   Second-degree burns usually heal without scars and without residual discomfort or pain. Why did the discomfort and tenderness last for three months after the blisters seemed to heal?

MF   These were very deep second-degree burns extending all the way through the epidermis to the superficial dermis, blood vessels, and nerves. I can illustrate what I mean by showing you a picture of the microscopic skin anatomy.

(He pulls out a large picture of the skin's appearance under a microscope.)

Most of the epidermis is composed of squamous cells. This is the layer (pointing to the picture), which is 4-7 cells deep. The lowest row of cells is known as the basal cell layer. This layer

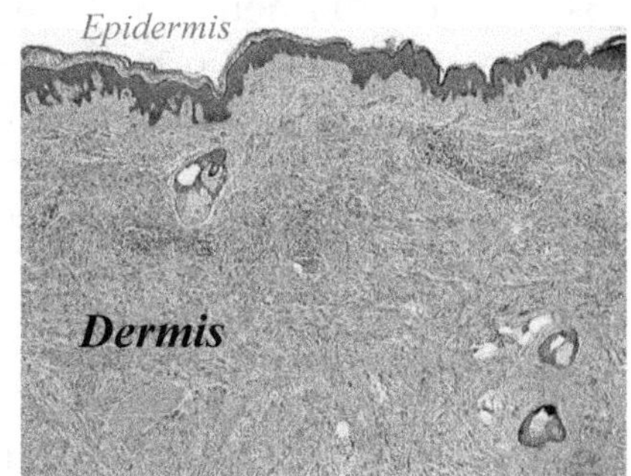

is composed of basal cells, but it also contains numerous pigment-forming cells called melanocytes (points to scattered melanocytes). Sunlight, ultraviolet A light, and ultraviolet B light stimulate the production of tan pigment. When ultraviolet A light shines on the skin, especially when combined with the ingestion of Psoralen, reddening is followed by a tanning response.

This combination causes the penetration of the light to go deep into the epidermis, where the melanocytes exist, and to penetrate even deeper into the upper portion of the dermis, where nerves and blood vessels are located. These superficial nerves and blood vessels are damaged. The damage to the vessels and to the epidermis causes the skin to turn red. Since nerve damage takes a long time to heal, pain and tenderness can persist for months, as it has for Mr. Motis, though the skin may appear healed. Because the intensity of the light reaching the melanocytes is intense, the tanning will be extreme.

JK   I have no further questions, your honor.

JC   Mr. Jones, would you like to question the witness?

GJ   No, your honor.

JC   In that case, we will recess until tomorrow morning at 10:00 a.m.

CC   Court is adjourned until 10 a.m. tomorrow morning.

(Tomorrow at 10 a.m. in court.)

JC   Mr. Jones, would you like to call your next witness?

GJ   Yes, your honor, Dr. John Peters.

(Dr. Peters comes up to the witness stand.)

CC   Dr. Peters, please place your right hand on the Bible. Do you
        swear to tell the truth, the whole truth, and nothing but the truth?

JP   I do.

GJ   Dr. Peters, what is your occupation?

JP   I am a board-certified dermatologist practicing in the state of New
        Jersey.

GJ   Have you ever treated Mr. Jack Motis for his skin condition?

JP   No, I am here as an expert witness.

GJ   Do you agree with Dr. Franklin's explanation as to why only his
        buttocks were burned with resultant blisters while the rest of his
        body, including his hips, and pubic area, turned pink with no
        blisters.

JP   I partially agree. The rest of his body, except for the hips, buttocks
        and pubic area, were already tan from the sun he had gotten in the
        Bahamas only a few weeks earlier. There can be only one
        explanation as to why he wasn't burned in those areas. He was
        bent forward at the waist, holding onto the handrails in the box.
        He was in a crouched position. His buttocks were much closer to
        the fluorescent lights behind him, while the pubic area was further
        away from the lights in front of him. The hips were where they

would have been if he had been standing straight, and that's why they didn't burn. The burns were not caused by giving him an improper light intensity.

(He illustrates Mr. Motis's standing position in the PUVA box.)

GJ   I have no further questions.

JC   Mr. Knight, do you wish to cross-examine the witness?

JK   Yes, your honor. Dr. Peters, do you have a PUVA lightbox in your office?

JP   No, I refer my patients who require treatment with PUVA to the University of Pennsylvania Dermatology Clinic.

JK   Then how can you consider yourself an expert witness?

JP   I go to the skin clinic at the University of Pennsylvania two afternoons a week to teach the residents. I show them how to give PUVA treatments for C-T-C-L, psoriasis, etc.

JK   Doctor, don't you make sure before you start these treatments that the patient understands that if they do not stand up straight, they overexpose certain areas of skin to excessive light radiation, which could lead to burns?

JP   Yes.

JK   Do you agree with Dr. Franklin's explanation of why patients with PUVA burns can take longer to heal?

JP   No. His description of the burn formation would lead to third-
      degree burns but not second-degree burns. Second-degree burns
      heal without pain or scarring in two weeks tops. Third-degree
      burns would wind up with visible scarring, which this patient does
      not have. A second-degree burn acts like a second-degree burn, no
      matter what the cause. He had second-degree burns, and with
      second-degree burns, there is no pain or discomfort after the burns
      heal.

JK   Thus, we have two differing opinions from the experts. Thank
      you, doctors. No further questions. Thank you, Dr. Peters. You
      may return to your seat.

GJ   Your honor, I would like to call Dr. Fine to the stand.

CC   Dr. Fine, please put your hand on the Bible. Do you swear to tell
      the truth, the whole truth, and nothing but the truth, so help me
      God?

(Dr. Fine put his hand on the Bible.)

AF   I do.

GJ   Dr. Fine, what is your occupation? Are you certified, and where
      did you get your training?

AF   I am a board-certified dermatologist. I trained at the hospital at the
      University of Pennsylvania.

GJ   How long have you been practicing dermatology?

AF   Thirty years.

GJ   How many years have you been treating patients with the PUVA box?

AF   Nine years.

GJ   Do your results warrant the risks?

AF   Patients with psoriasis, vitiligo, and cutaneous T-cell lymphoma do very well with PUVA treatments. It is a safer and more effective modality than any other treatment.

GJ   Do you tell patients about possible side effects?

AF   Either I do, or my physician's assistant does.

GJ   Was Mr. Motis told about possible side effects, including second-degree burns?

AF   Cynthia Wils, my physician's assistant, told him about the possible side effects and instructed him on how they might be prevented.

GJ   Did he follow her instructions?

AF   Obviously not, or he would not have had the blisters he had.

GJ   Whose fault was it that he had the burns, yours or his?

AF   We gave him instructions, which he failed to follow.

GJ   I have no further questions.

JC   Mr. Knight, would you like to cross-examine the witness?

JK   Yes, your honor. Dr. Fine, were you in the room when Ms. Wils spoke with Mr. Motis?

AF   That's her job, and she is very reliable.

JK   Please answer the question. Did you see or hear her give the patient instructions? Yes or no?

AF   No.

JK   What you have stated then is 100% conjecture. You were not in the room at the time, and you really don't know what was said or what wasn't said. Is that true? Yes or no?

AF   Yes

JC   Please call the next witness.

JK   I would like to call Mrs. Motis to the stand.

(Mrs. Motis takes the witness chair, is given the Bible, and places her right hand on it.)

CC   Mrs. Motis, do you swear to tell the truth, the whole truth, and nothing but the truth, so help you God?

AM   I do.

JK   Mrs. Motis, how long had you been married to Mr. Motis when he developed his skin condition?

AM   About two months.

JK   Was this the first marriage for both of you?

AM   No, this was the second marriage for both of us.

JK   And were you having normal marital relations?

AM   Yes, Mr. Motis and I were having normal marital relations for
      about eight months when those horrible burns were inflicted by
      Dr. Fine. I'm 52 years old, and he is only 56 years old.

JK   And after the burns, you could no longer have normal sexual
      relations?

GJ   I object, your honor.

JC   Sustained. Mr. Knight ask the question. Don't give her the
      answer.

JK   After the burns were inflicted, were you able to have normal
      relations?

AM   No. He couldn't lie on his back. He was in too much pain.

JK   I have no more questions, your honor.

JC   Mr. Jones, would you like to question the witness?

GJ   Yes, your honor. Mrs. Motis, you say he was lying on his back
      during sex? Could you describe your position during intercourse?

JK   I object. This is a very personal and embarrassing matter.

(Whispering, soft talk, and soft laughter in the courtroom.)

JC   Quiet in the court, or I will empty the courtroom.

AM   That's all right, Judge. I don't mind answering the question. I'm not shy.

GJ   Men are usually on top, and women are on the bottom. If Mr. Motis is on top, why was he getting back pains?

JK   I object.

JC   Objection overruled. Answer the question.

AM   We like to start lovemaking by having oral sex. Jack has to be on his back. He can't be on top of me. Then we like to rest for maybe a half hour. Then I get on top of him, and you know - we make love. Jack is always on the bottom. I have a slipped disc problem and really can't be on the bottom or on my side, only on top.

GJ   That's why Mr. Motis can't be on top? You have a slipped disc, and that's why you can't be on the bottom, and when Mr. Motis had burns on his butt, neither of you could be on the bottom? This is a very complicated situation. I have no further questions.

JC   Are there any other witnesses?

GJ   Your honor, Mrs. Cynthia Wils Cohen will be coming in tomorrow morning or early afternoon from Miami to testify. She was Dr. Fine's physician's assistant who spoke to Mr. Motis about possible side effects from the treatments.

JC   In that case, we will adjourn for today and reconvene tomorrow at 11 a.m. Court is adjourned.

(Paul Shalita on the phone to Dr. Fine at his office the next morning.)

PS   Al, I haven't spoken to you since your trial began. What's
        happening?

AF   It's not going well. It's like they know every move we are going to
        make. When we showed the medical release in the courtroom, the
        attorney for Mr. Motis objected, claiming that it was an illegal
        document. We should have titled it "Informed Consent" instead of
        "Medical Release." He claimed that a medical release takes away
        the patient's right to sue the doctor. We can't deprive him of that
        right legally.

PS   That's bull. He did sue you, didn't he? It doesn't take away the
        right to sue. It diminishes the chance of the plaintiff winning the
        suit. It protects the doctor, and that is legal. Didn't your attorney
        challenge him? A medical release and an informed consent are
        essentially the same things. They tell the patient that there are
        certain risks that accompany the treatments, and if you accept
        these risks, you are allowing or releasing the doctor to give you
        these treatments. If you don't accept those risks in writing and
        won't sign, the doctor doesn't want the risk of treating you. Why
        should he risk being sued?

AF   The Judge told the jury that the release was not a legal document.
        My attorney was an idiot and did not challenge the ruling. The
        jury was told to disregard everything that was in the release and
        act as if it never existed. He told us never to refer to it again.

PS   Did your lawyer then ask you to contact Cynthia and ask her to come testify?

AF   Originally, he said the release would be sufficient. She would not have to appear as a witness. Actually, Cynthia had moved to Miami to be with her husband. She was the one who had given Motis all the information about the disease, the treatments, and the problems that could arise from the treatments. His lawyer keeps saying that I spent little time with Mr. Motis. He never mentions the time that Cynthia spent with him going over everything. We were not allowed to mention the medical release he signed. That would have proven that he clearly understood the dangers and how to avoid them.

PS   You must get Cynthia to come here and testify.

AF   I know. As soon as I heard the Judge say that we could not refer to the medical release, I tried to reach her. Two years ago she married a guy from Miami. His last name was Cohen. Do you know how many Cohens there are in the Miami phone book? Cynthia did not list her name in the phone book, so after two days and 79 phone calls, I finally contacted her. Her husband's first name is Zachery, and we called all the Cohens in alphabetical order. I spoke to her yesterday morning, and the first flight she could get out of Miami was today at 10:00 a.m., so we will see her around 1:30 p.m.

PS   Call me tomorrow and let me know what happens.

AF   OK. Bye.

PS   Bye.

AF   Wait, I have one more question. At one point, I was going to ask
       the Judge if I could get rid of Jones and represent myself.

PS   It's a good thing you didn't. If you had lost your case, your
       insurance company would refuse to pay the damages. You would
       be totally responsible.

AF   That is what I thought might happen. Bye.

PS   By the way, what did your lawyer say when you told him that you
       were trying to contact Cynthia?

AF   Nothing. He just looked at me funny.

PS   Hmm! Bye.

(That day in courtroom – 11:00 a.m.)

JC   Mr. Jones, has Mrs. Wils-Cohen arrived?

GJ   No, your honor. Her plane has been delayed, but she should be
       here no later than 2:00 p.m.

JC   Let's continue with the summations. I really can't wait. I'm
       scheduled to begin a new case in two days, and we are already
       running behind here. I thought it would be finished entirely by
       now.

AF   (Whispers to GJ) Can't we ask the Judge to wait until 3:00 p.m.?

GJ   I'll go ask him.

(GJ and JC speak in low tones.)

GJ   (To AF) He won't wait.

AF   (Speaking to himself), I wonder what he really asked him.

(The summations begin.)

JC   Mr. Knight.

JK   Ladies and gentlemen of the jury. You have heard the facts. Mr.
        Motis is referred to Dr. Fine for a cancerous skin rash, which
        requires a special physician who is an expert in giving PUVA light
        treatments. Instead of being treated by his physician, he is seen
        and treated by a physician's assistant who is not a dermatologist.
        She is not a physician. As a result, the patient suffers severe burns
        over parts of his body. This results in him not being able to go to
        work. He cannot have normal sexual relations with his wife of
        only several months. He suffers monetary losses, which force him
        to sell his home and move into a small apartment. He is fired by
        two banks that have employed him as a real estate appraiser. His
        whole life has been turned topsy-turvy. She has given him a super
        strong fluorescent light treatment without giving him proper
        supervision. He tells us that Dr. Fine didn't have time to supervise
        his case. He was in too much of a hurry. Dr. Franklyn, the
        dermatologist who acted as the expert witness for Mr. Motis, says
        that Dr. Fine caused the burns because he never gave proper

instructions as to how or where to stand in relation to the light bulbs. He never told him to stand straight or to hold onto the handrails. Members of the jury, consider all these facts when you leave the courtroom to reach your verdict.

(JK returns to his seat.)

JC   Mr. Jones - your summation.

GJ   Ladies and gentlemen of the jury, my client, Dr. Fine, is a well-respected dermatologist in the Philadelphia and Abington areas. He is on the staff at a hospital at the University of Pennsylvania. There was a physician's assistant, Cynthia Wils, who had been working for Dr. Fine for 20 years. She gave the treatment and, together with the light treatment, full instructions. Two years ago, she got married and moved to Miami, Florida. We tried but could not locate her so she might appear here as a witness.

JC   Mr. Jones, you are not giving us a proper summation of the facts. Tell us what happened during the treatment, not what didn't happen. Please proceed.

GJ   I have nothing further to say, your honor.

JC   Members of the jury, please return to the jury room to discuss the case and to reach a verdict. We will convene again at that time.

(Cynthia Wils Cohen arrives at the courtroom, but too late. Her testimony is no longer accepted.)

AF   I'm sorry, Cynthia, that I didn't reach out to you earlier. I know
        you would have been a great witness. However, Diane and I want
        you to visit with us for a few days.

(AF and CW walk out of the courtroom together talking softly.)

(Next morning.)

JC   I understand the jury has reached a verdict. Bailiff, please bring
        them back into the courtroom.

(Jury reenters and takes their seats.)

JC   I understand that you have reached a verdict.

JURY LEADER Yes, your honor. The jury finds the defendant, Dr.
        Allen Fine, liable on all counts and awards the following
        settlements:

To Mr. Motis - $300,000 for pain and suffering and loss of income and
        $25,000 for loss of consortium. To Mrs. Motis - $25,000 for loss
        of consortium.

JC   (Repeats the verdict.) Thank you. Any questions? No, then I
        would like to thank Mr. Knight and Mr. Jones and invite them to
        meet with me in my chambers at 12 noon today. Court is
        adjourned.

(As Dr. Fine leaves the court room, he sees George Jones talking softly on the phone. Jones hangs up the phone quickly when he sees Dr. Fine.)

AF   Mr. Jones do think we could appeal this verdict to a higher court?

GJ   On what grounds?

AF   That means no, right?

GJ   Right.

(Two months later, in Dr. Fine's office. Mrs. Binswanger comes into the office.)

AF   Well, we just completed a thorough skin exam, and I didn't see anything that looked suspicious. If there are any moles or growths that you don't like, we can remove and biopsy them. Otherwise, you are free to go.

MB   I will see you in a year.

AF   Oh, by the way, you work for the law firm Block and Shore, don't you?

MB   Yes. I'm in charge of the billing department. We have 29 lawyers in the firm, so we need a billing department.

AF   Did you know a lawyer there by the name of Joseph Knight?

MB   Sure. Why?

AF   Just asking. Have you ever heard of a lawyer named George Jones?

MB   Yes. He's really good friends with the head of the legal department, Mr. Jordan. They went to law school together. They graduated in the top 10% of their class. He doesn't belong to our firm, but when we get really busy and need extra lawyers, we call on him to help us out. Just two months ago, I gave him a large check for a case he had just completed.

AF   (Gives Mrs. Binswanger a strange look.) That's interesting. Say hello for me next time you see him.

MB   OK. See you in a year.

(She leaves the office.)

AF   That son of a bitch.

(Next day. Dr. Fine calls Paul Shalita.)

AF   The woman who is head of the billing department at Block and Shore, the firm that accused me, came in to see me as a patient yesterday. She essentially told me that they planted Jones in with my insurance company by putting in the lowest bid for his services at the trial.

PS   That does not surprise me. It's over. Forget it.

AF   Paul, before you hang up, I want to get deeper into my thoughts about the case. First, what did you think about their lawyer?

PS   I thought that Joe Knight was a very clever and shrewd attorney. He had several things that he had to do. He did them well, and he did them all. His main objective was to get rid of the medical release. That in itself would have betrayed their whole case. Without planting their attorney for the defense, they would never have been able to void the medical release. They claimed that the release was an illegal document because it did not permit the patient to sue his or her physician. That in itself is ridiculous. They had sued you, hadn't they? Any honest and decent lawyer would have issued a strong and legal challenge to that claim. Jones issued no challenge. If such a document were illegal, it would serve no purpose, and thus it would not exist. Actually, the terms "medical release" and "informed consent" are identical. The differences are miniscule.

George Jones did not want Cynthia to testify. He told you that the medical release would suffice. There would be no need to bring Cynthia in as a witness. He knew full well that the release was going to be thrown out of court.

AF   What would have happened if Cynthia had happened to arrive at court in time to testify?

PS   Jones would not have been happy, but I am sure he had made contingency plans. First, he would have asked her very few questions trying to get her off the witness stand as quickly as possible. Knight would have asked her if there were any other people in the room with her and Mr. Motis at the time she gave the instructions to him. You told me that they were not. Motis said she gave him a piece of paper to sign – the medical release, but no instructions. It's her word against his. She told him that if he didn't sign it, he would not be given the treatments at that office.

AF   If I had a decent lawyer, what would he have done?

PS   A decent lawyer would have suspected that Motis might lie. The lawyer would have had former patients who had been given PUVA light treatments appear as witnesses. He would ask them whether you or Cynthia had given them adequate warnings about possible side effects and what they might do to avoid these side effects. George Jones was not about to be a decent lawyer.

AF   What about the fact that Motis's 1995 income tax return showed that he didn't have to pay taxes that year?

PS   Interesting point. Motis stated that because of prolonged pain, he had to lessen his work schedule severely. He pointed out that he had to sell his house and move into a small apartment. But he never showed his tax returns for that year to the jury. Was he trying to hide something? Could there have been a huge financial loss in another business with which he was involved? If I were Knight, and everything was on the up and up, I wouldn't hesitate to show those returns. George Jones told you he had the returns, but he never offered to show them to you, did he? You should have asked to see them. Allen, I never mentioned this to you, but I think you may have been set up by Mr. and Mrs. Motis. I believe he lost a lot of money in another business. When Cynthia told them how to avoid getting burned in the PUVA box, she also told him how he could get burned by putting his rear end close to the ultraviolet bulbs. He figured that if he got burned, he could sue you and get back some of his lost money. I can't prove that, but I would not put it past him.

AF	I'll bet you are right. Why do you think that Knight waited until the last minute to appeal the decision of the Arbitration panel and bring the case to the Court of Common Pleas?

PS	He wanted to make sure that all his chess pieces were in order. He knew that Amalgamated Protective Insurance Company picked the cheapest lawyer they could find to defend their client. The longer he waited, the more certain he became that George Jones would be their man. If any other insurance company had defended you, the case would never have gone to the Court of Common Pleas.

AF	Do you think that Judge Clark was in on the fix?

PS	I don't know, but I don't think so.

AF	Then why wouldn't he allow more time for Cynthia to get here before sending the jury out to render a verdict?

PS	You were not in on the conversation between Jones and the Judge. He may not have brought up Cynthia at all. For all you know, he could have been inviting the Judge over to his house for dinner, or maybe he told the Judge that she wasn't coming to testify.

AF   Do you think Mr. and Mrs. Motis were lying about their inability
        to have sex because of his burns?

PS   Why not? They lied when they said that Cynthia did not go over
        the possible side effects of PUVA and how to avoid them. They
        lied when they said the pain in the buttock area lasted 2-3 months.
        I think that she lied when she claimed that she had a herniated
        disc, which forced her to be on top when they had sex, etc., etc.,
        etc. I think that they don't know how to tell the truth and that
        Knight coached them very well.

AF   Those dirty bastards. When I retire, I'm going to write a play,
        maybe a movie, and show the country how the legal system works
        in Philadelphia. Maybe I'll have Tom Hanks play the role of Dr.
        Allen Fine!

THE END

AUTHORS

Dr. Joseph Shrager

ADVISORS

Diane Shrager

Carole Albrecht

Paul Shalita - legal advisor

www.ingramcontent.com/pod-product-compliance
Lightning Source LLC
Chambersburg PA
CBHW060601100726

47907CB00005B/1466